This Book
BELONGS to
Sisters
Sienna + Tia xo♡ox

ISBN 0-8249-8676-8

Published by Riverton Press

Distributed by Ideals Publications
535 Metroplex Drive, Suite 250
Nashville, Tennessee 37211
www.idealsbooks.com

Text copyright © 2006 by Mark Kimball Moulton
Art copyright © 2006 by Karen Hillard Good

Color separations by Precision Color Graphics,
Franklin, Wisconsin

Printed and bound in Italy by LEGO

10 9 8 7 6 5 4 3 2 1

Designed by Georgina Chidlow-Rucker

We (Karen and Mark)
would like to
whole-heartedly thank
our batty families and friends
that we cherish with
all of our
♡ hearts! ♡

Twisted Sistahs

The true story of the first Halloween... honest!

Written by Mark Kimball Moulton

Art by Karen Hillard Good

Riverton Press

One-hundred-thousand years ago and twenty miles away,

there lived three sistahs known to be
most **gorgeous** in their day.

They had the kind of beauty
only read about in books,

and everyone across the land
was taken with their looks.

The oldest was TALLULAH-ROSE,
the second, AGNES-BEULAH.

The third, and loveliest of all,
was JEZEBEL-PECULIAH.

Now, though the girls were beautiful,
they hardly looked the same~

some said the only thing they shared
was GHOULYAH, their last name.

You've got mail.

ghoulyah

The Original
Red Hat girls

TALLULAH-ROSE had raven hair and green skin,
  like a lizard,
which she maintained with nightly masks
  of puréed chicken gizzards.

  AGNES-BEULAH was quite tall and statuesque-ly thin,
  and she **always** kept the whiskers braided on her pretty chin.

  And JEZEBEL-PECULIAH . . . aaahhh . . .
mere words cannot describe her~

  her looks made men fall to their knees
  and shook their very fiber.
She was **such** a roly-poly thing~as round as a balloon~
and her lovely, iridescent face was wrinkled, like a prune.

Her hair hung like a nest of snakes, the color like no other~
  a drop-dead shade of pumpkin-red

  they **say** came from her mother.
  (H-m-m-m-m . . .)

  But if I had to choose one thing,
  her most **attractive** feature,
  I'd say it was her eyebrow that
  looked like some furry creature.

  It crawled across her forehead from the
  far left to the right,
  and it wiggled when she flirted~
a most
  captivating
  sight.

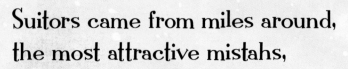

Suitors came from miles around,
the most attractive mistahs,

each vying for one moment with those lovely GHOULYAH sistahs.

Counts and kings and firemen and every grand marquis,
would wait for countless **days** to date one of the lovely three.

The girls would peek, coquettishly, from upstairs in their house,
evaluating all the men for a potential spouse~

"Ooooo, look at him, how handsome! And what dreamy bright red eyes.
And that one there-how debonair.
Just watch how he can fly!"

For all those handsome suitors,
all those men who came to court,

were distinguished, (or extinguished),
and a **most** distinctive sort.

By now, it must seem obvious~the girls were in a pickle . . .

how could they choose just **one** of them and not appear too fickle?

So they put their heads together and decided on a plan~

they'd throw a giant party and they'd invite every man!

They'd calculate, evaluate, appraise, assess, and judge~

and determine **then** which of those men deserved to get the nudge.

Oh, they were just delighted, those three lovely GHOULYAH gals~
then AGNES, dear, said, "Why stop there? Let's invite all our pals!"

Well . . . talk about excited~those three girls were in a tizzy!
They knew they had so much to do, they really must get busy.

First they checked the calendar, deciding on a date~
Mid-December or November? Heavens, that was much too late!

"H-m-m-m, how about October?" offered MISS TALULLAH-ROSE,
as she rubbed the hairy wart that graced her elegant, long nose.

"Why, yes! Perhaps the 31st," suggested AGNES-BEULAH.
"Oh, I love it!" cried the darling little JEZEBEL-PECULIAH~

"So many of our dearest friends just float around that night,
and our party will afford the perfect time to reunite!"

So they made a big, ol' "X" mark through October thirty-first,
then consulted their address book and they soon became immersed.

With playful shrieks and cackles
they just flew from A to Z,
inviting everyone they knew,
both friends and family.

They wrote the invitations out on pink construction paper,
describing every detail of their late October caper.

Then they folded up those precious notes with concentrated care,
and they took them to the roof and **wheee!** sent them flying through the air!

A million little paper planes went soaring out that day,
heading north, south, east, and west and every other way.

Now all that there was left to do was cook and **maybe** clean,
and save at least a week or two to powder, primp, and preen.

They fried up lots of spider legs,

then made fresh frog's egg soup~

black beetle pies and deviled eyes and other slimy goop.
(M-mm-mm-mm, M-m-m-m!)

They decided that the cleaning of the house would **have** to wait,

or they'd **never** have sufficient time preparing for their dates.

Manicures and pedicures, massages, tints, and curls~

it's hard work, you know, to look as lovely as those lovely girls.

They tried on **gobs** of make-up~

lipstick, rouge, and false eyelashes~

Then modeled different hats and cloaks

and gowns with long black sashes.

Fried Bat Wings

Slimey Goop Punch

Apple Cider

They stood before their mirror
with both hands upon their hips,
just fluttering their gorgeous eyes and puckering their lips.

TALLULAH-ROSE looked mahh-velous~ her green skin was just glowing,
and MISS AGNES-BEULAH'S whiskers were luxuriant and flowing.

But JEZEBEL-PECULIAH, aaahhh,
now she was one true vision,
(although she gave the credit
to her talented beautician) . . .

Her eyebrow was SO fluffy
it looked like a squirrel's tail,

and she had a different polish painted
on each different nail!

Her stringy orange hair stood straight
out from her wrinkled face,

and she wore a dab
of skunk-cabbage for scent,
but
    juuust
        a trace.

mummy

She had put on a pound
(or twelve)
to add to her allure,

and her roly-poly figure
just **demanded** "haute couture."

Her dress was simply stunning~
a floor length black canvas tent,

with room for six cats underneath
to follow where she went.

She **threw** tradition to the wind~
forwent the pointed hat~

and instead she wore a halo
of her favorite pets~live bats!

Now normally the sistahs
were without a jealous care,

but sweet JEZEBEL-PECULIAH'S
look was more than
they could bear.

But putting jealousy aside
(though they could hardly bear it,)

they knew that girl had fashion sense
and she could really wear it!

"Please, Pleeease, oh, darling sistah,"
they both asked, they begged,
they pleaded~

"Won't you puh-leeze
take a good look at us
and tell us what is needed?"

So JEZEBEL-PECULIAH
put a finger to her chin,
stepped back and thought a minute,
then said~
"Girls~you're waaay too thin . . ."

"But come, my gaunt faced dearies.
Let's just see what we can do~
I'm sure I must have
something
that is suitable
for you."

She opened up her closet door
and stuck her head inside,

reached past a dusty skeleton
and pushed two more aside.

"Why, **here,**" said lovely JEZEBEL,
"let's see how **this** might look,"

and she gingerly removed a boa
hanging from a hook.

It was perfect for TALLULAH,
complimenting her green skin,

and MISS AGNES-BEULAH borrowed her
new cape of eel fins.

Oh, yes, **now** the girls were ready
for their swank affair that night,

and if I may,
I'd like to say,
they all looked
out-a sight!

. . . **and** just in time,
for as our beauties

sashayed down the stairs,
fluffing up the spider webs

that graced their lovely hairs,
the doorbell rang

and on their
porch . . .

were forty-hundred men,
all clamoring to be the first to get a look at them.

(Weeell . . . maybe I exaggerate, but I tell ya, there were lots~
poets, doctors, lawyers, even Hollywood hot-shots!)

Luckily, the GHOULYAH gals had thought to hire IGOR~
 a man of many talents
  who stood nearly eight-foot-four.

DING!
DONG!

So all the men were **veeery nice**
 who lined up at their door,
 'cause it was clearly obvious~
**You do NOT mess
with IGOR!**

Giggling, the sistahs checked
 the mirror one last time,
 then lined up in the foyer
 as the clock began to chime.

Bong! Bong! Bong!
Bong! Bong! Bong!
Bong! Bong! Bong!
Bong! Bong! Bong!

Royally, TALLULAH
 nodded once to start the band,
 then IGOR opened up the door
 at AGNES' command.

One by one their guests arrived,
 announced by IGOR'S bellow,
 accompanied by harpsichords
 and ancient screeching cellos.

The sistahs were so gracious
with each guest that they received,
and some of them
who came that night
you wouldn't have believed!

COUNT DRACULA and his best friend, a dentist down the street,
arrived with many goodies they laid at the GHOULYAH'S feet.

There were shovels, picks, and axes, and a large, sharp wooden spike,
a coffin lined with purple silk and a bright blue mountain bike!

FRANKENSTEIN stomped in
and brought a beautiful bouquet,
of wilted flowers grouped around
a poison ivy spray.

The girls were tickled pink with
these 'cause everybody knows,

the way to **any** girl's heart's with flowers

. . . or with clothes.

(. . . or shoes.)

(. . . or chocolate.)

JACK and JILL O'LANTERN
made their entrance on a raven,

while belting out show tunes like "MAME"
and yes, "AIN'T MISBEHAVIN'"!

Oh, what a gay, ol' couple,
always grinning ear to ear-

just absolutely **radiant**
and full of fun and cheer.

They did a routine tap dance
and a bit of Vaudeville "shtick,"

and for treats, they brought
carved pumpkins
to be used as candlesticks.

(How clever!)

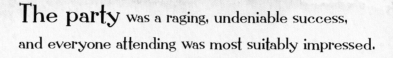

The party was a raging, undeniable success,
and everyone attending was most suitably impressed.

The music was delightful, performed by
THE SCAREAWACKIES,
whose singer called herself "the artist
formerly known as BLACKIE."

Years ago they made the charts with
"MIDNIGHT SCREAMS" and "SCREECHES,"
but their most famous song to date
was "SUCKING FACE WITH LEACHES."

They had the whole crowd on their feet~
they danced the whole night long~
calling out for "More! More! More!"
right after every song.

The harpsichord was dynamite,
the clicking bones kept rhythm~
and when they sang "SWEET CEMETERY LOVE"
everybody joined in with 'em.

The food was simply scrumptious~

almost sinfully delicious~

fit for kings and counts and queens and mummys, ghouls, and witches.

(They **did** run out of spider legs but no one seemed to mind~

they just fried up some fresh rat tails, all that the girls could find.)

Everyone loved **all** the games

planned by those lovely sistahs~

(except that bad WITCH OF THE EAST~

she hated playing "Twistah.")

They bobbed for apples (green ones with worms,)

and then played Blind-Man's-Bluff,

Spin-the-Femur, Charades, and Tag,

and lotsa other stuff.

Oh, yes, those scintillating girls sure could throw one great bash,

and everyone agreed that night~those girls just **oozed** panache.

Now, the purpose of this whole affair, if you'll remember, friends,

was so that those enchanting girls could choose between those mens.

Well, I hate to be a gossip,
I don't tell tales out-a-school,
but those men that night were so bewitched
they acted just like fools!

They dogged MISS AGNES-BEULAH everywhere that poor girl went,
and they pestered dear, sweet JEZEBEL in her black canvas tent.

But the most sought after sistah was genteel TALLULAH-ROSE~
there was not one man who could resist that wart upon her nose.

So the sistahs slipped away and fled up to their widows walk,
to fix their make-up, catch their breath, and have a little talk.

"Well! Goodness gracious! Me, oh, my!"
        gasped those poor, worn out sistahs~
"Who knew it would be so much work
        to fend off all those mistahs!"

They slumped against the railing
        and decided there and then . . .

        if **this** was how their lives would be,
            they didn't need no men!

                        But stiiill. . .

They did love the attention all those handsome men bestowed,
(though they laughingly suggested they should turn 'em into toads).

So our three girls decided
on that same day, every year,
they'd go all out,
invite their friends
and hold a shindig there!

hee hee
hee hee
hee...

Their soiree became a grand event,
folks just **died** to make the scene.
It was put on every calendar
and they called it "HALLOWEEN!"

Soon **everywhere** around the world,
in every land and nation,
folks began to hold their own
October celebration.

Now, you may call it jealousy
or simple affectation,
but **everyone** aspired to match
the GHOULYAH'S adoration.

Folks would wear a plastic wart with hair upon their nose,
attempting to look like the glamorous TALLULAH-ROSE.

Others donned a stringy wig of reddish-orange hair,
trying to capture JEZEBEL-PECULIAH'S "savoir-faire."

Designers clambered for the right to market her black tent,
and to be the first to bottle her unique skunk-cabbage scent.

("JEZEBEL" became the most desired scent to wear~
the signature fragrance of cultured women, everywhere!)

Soon it was the "thing to do" to dress for Halloween,
as a "GHOULYAH" or a goblin
or a count or king or queen.

And so it has continued up until this very day,
that we celebrate each Halloween
    the "GHOULYAH sistah way!"

We carve our pumpkins carefully
and light them with bright candles~
(hoping that they won't be smashed
by creepy, little vandals)~

And we dress as mummys, ghouls, and ghosts
of souls long since departed,
emulating what the lovely
GHOULYAH sistahs started.

Though none so far can hold a match
to AGNES or TALLULAH,
nor capture the true essence of
sweet JEZEBEL-PECULIAH . . .

The beauty of the GHOULYAH girls
is still the aspiration,
of every fresh-faced little girl
across this great, big nation.

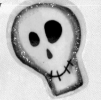

Come Closer
if You DaRe!

BeWaRe!

I'll
save
You!

RIP

mY
hero!

But I'm sure that some of you who have been sitting with me here, wonder how I know so much about that first affair.....
Well, perhaps You won't believe me but each word is true, I swear~ and I tell You in all honesty... I know cause.....

Sweet Treats: Sierra+Tia!